Secrets, Lies, & CHOCOLATE CHIP COOKIES

RECIPES TO DIE FOR

TIERNEY JAMES

Publishing Coordinator – Sharon Kizziah-Holmes
Cover Design by Sweet 'N Spicy Designs

PRESS

Owasso, OK

ISBN - 978-1-965460-35-1 (Paperback)
ISBN - 978-1-965460-36-8 (eBook)

DEDICATION

This book is dedicated to the Southern women who have always taught me about cooking and fed me the best meals a person could want. Thank you to these amazing cooks.

Marie Johnson – my mom
Zelma Johnson – grandmother
Lena Cooke – grandmother
Martha Ervin – aunt
Peggy Hunter – aunt

CONTENTS

INTRODUCTION

When I began talking to the agents at Enigma about a possible cookbook, they were not 100 percent behind the project. Since they work in the shadows and most everything they do is classified, the thought of putting something on paper that others might read and connect to them, left the group feeling a little exposed. Once I told them it was for Tessa Scott and that I had cleared it with Director Benjamin Clark, they were more responsive.

Although this is not your typical cookbook with page after page of recipes, this one gives you narrative from the agents that can be snarky and revealing at times. In real life they battle the elements and people that would harm our country. Tessa is the one thing that not only keeps them grounded, but has become the glue that holds them together. When I say they are a team, the truth is they have become a family.

Yes, there seems to be some kind of affection toward Tessa when it comes to Captain Chase Hunter, although he rejects that evaluation. She too, has been known to make rash decisions only because the mighty captain asked her to do it. The other players on the team and at Enigma, have different roles. If you want to know more about them, start with the book *An Unlikely Hero*. All the books are standalone, but now that the team has been together for several years you might want to know some of the background chaos that has thrown them together.

Many of the recipes will be given by the agents, along with myself. They will share a little about why a particular recipe was included on their behalf. There will be moments you may laugh out loud or rush to make the concoction they listed. Either way, this is probably the first cookbook that is meant, to not only give good food choices, but to entertain the heck out of you.

Tierney James

CONTRIBUTORS

The following people donated recipes to make this book happen.

Author Shirley McCann
Author Willy Robbins
Author Caroline Giammanco
Gwen Guymon
John & Cindy Johnson
John & Melinda Tierney
Deb Gromer
Tierney James

Enigma Characters
Tessa Scott
Captain Chase Hunter
Roman Darya Petrov
Nicholas Zoric
Samantha Cordova
Carter Johnson
Vernon Kemp
Honey Lynch
Director Benjamin Clark
FBI Agent Dennis Martin
President Buck Austin
Martha & Francis Ervin
Agent Willy Robbins
Dr. Wu
Under Secretary of State Bonnie Finley
Army Ranger Lieutenant Ken Montgomery
Marine Gunnery Sergeant Tom Cooper
Tessa's kids – Sean Patrick, Daniel, Heather

WHO IS TESSA SCOTT?

Secrets, Lies, & Chocolate Chip Cookies

My name is Tessa Scott and I'm a liar. Not by choice of course. I have been forced into this predicament because of being in the wrong place at the wrong time, my home. Now I pretend to be something that I used to be before "they" took over my life, before Captain Hunter made me second guess everything I believed to be true and just, in this world. My friend, Tierney James, said it would be therapeutic to write this. I'm not sure my real therapist would agree. Yes, I have a therapist. Once I begin my story, you'll understand why I need someone sane to confess my sins. Besides. I didn't have a choice. Everyone at my day job is mandated to visit Dr. Wu. But I'm getting ahead of myself.

I'm a happily married woman with three kids, two boys and a girl. I live in a beautiful Victorian farm house in Grass Valley, California. My husband is a lawyer and I'm a teacher. Or at least I was until Enigma got involved. Now I live a secret life that parallels my pretend life. I swear I didn't have a choice!

It started when Captain Chase Hunter forced his way into my house after the rest of my family left on vacation. He lied to me from the first moment we met. Considering he saved my life twice that day, I forgave him. I also started down a perilous road of hero worship. Maybe that's why I do it. Our friendship turned into a complicated relationship that jeopardizes any happiness with my husband Robert. If he ever finds out what I've done in the name of national security he'll either divorce or kill me.

I'm already feeling like I shouldn't have started this story to tell you about my life. I'll continue if you are interested in what I do. Sometimes I'll have to just write about my day or what the kids are doing. But mostly I need to tell you the shameful things I've stooped to doing in the name of freedom.

BREAKFAST & BRUNCH

Breakfast & Brunch Actors

Tessa Scott – A reluctant agent forced into service by President Buck Austin. After saving his life during a hurricane in Washington DC, he decides to manipulate her into being an advisor on cultural affairs. Her knowledge in world geography cements her place at Enigma.

Captain Chase Hunter – He is the leader for this Enigma team. He has a Ph.D. in literature and speaks five languages. After graduating from West Point, he became an Army Ranger and later a Delta Force officer. Until Tessa stumbled into his life, he was considered a cold-hearted man that no job was too dirty for him to finish when it came to national security.

Robert Scott – Lawyer by trade, he's also Tessa's husband who is clueless at what she does when he isn't around. The Enigma team find him shallow and a worthy kill, but refrain from taking action because of promises to protect him on her behalf. Although a good man, he is self-absorbed and finds it difficult to be the kind of father and husband Tessa needs. It will be his downfall.

Martha Ervin – Having worked as an agent for Enigma off and on for years, she now has moved next door to the Scott family to help with managing her household and children while she is on a mission. She is like a loving grandmother to the children. Tessa understands that if trouble should arise with another terrorist incident in her home, Martha can handle the situation with extreme prejudice.

Mini Quiche Recipe (Tessa)

I love this for Sunday brunch. Add a salad and it tastes like you spent way too much time in the kitchen. I usually make several different kinds because my kids eat like Marines who have just come back from combat maneuvers.

Ingredients

1 pie crust	Chopped ham
6 large eggs	Chopped broccoli
1 c. heavy cream	Bacon cooked & crumbled
1 ½ c. grated cheddar cheese	Garlic minced or onion
Salt & Pepper	Seafood cooked & chopped
Pinch of cayenne pepper is optional	Chopped green bell pepper
Add ins: You choose	
Chopped spinach	

Instructions

Preheat oven 375. Spray mini muffin tin with nonstick cooking spray, set aside (I used regular muffin tins.) Use small round cutter, cut pie crust and place into indentations of muffin tin and place in the oven to pre-bake for about 15 minutes. Whisk together eggs and heavy cream until light and fluffy. Add salt, pepper, and cayenne pepper, until well-combined. Stir in cheese. Pour into pie shells and top with add-in options as desired. Bake for 15-25 minutes until the egg mix is set. Remove from the oven and let rest about 5 minutes before serving.

I combined things. You can make your own toppings.

No Man Left Behind Breakfast Casserole (Captain Chase Hunter)

Forget feeding me and my men quiche and fruity whatever for breakfast. We need food that will stick to your ribs. In my line of work you never know when you might get to eat again. Might as well make it count first thing in the morning.

Ingredients

Melt 1 T. butter in bottom of 9 x 13 pan
Add ½ pkg. of (28 oz.) Potatoes O'Brian in pan
Add 1 lb. browned sausage
2 c. grated cheddar or cheddar jack cheese
Then add the remaining ½ pkg of potatoes.
Salt & pepper to taste

Instructions

Mix 1 dozen beaten eggs with ¼ c. milk, then pour on top of everything.

Bake 45 minutes at 350 degrees. Then add another 1 cup cheese on top. Return to oven for another 15 minutes.

Breakfast Sliders (Tessa)

This is my compromise for those agents who think they have to chow down on meaty casseroles for breakfast. Not only is it a fast fix, it's delicious.

Ingredients

1 pkg. Hawaiian rolls
Slices of ham
Swiss or Mozzarella cheese slices
Poppy seeds
¾ c. Melted butter.

Instructions

Slice Hawaiian rolls in half, placing the bottoms in a 9 x13 pan. Top with ham and cheese. Replace tops. Pour melted butter over all the sandwiches and then sprinkle poppy seeds over the top. Bake in 350 degrees oven until cheese melts. About 10-15 minutes. Remove and serve. Left overs can be warmed up for lunch. Caution: Don't eat the poppy seeds if your next stop is to take a drug test. It might not turn out well for you. I'm just saying.

Breads & Cereals

Homeland Pizza Crust (Robert – the husband)

I'm not sure why Tierney James and Tessa named this recipe 'Homeland' unless it's because I make it at home. Sometimes I feel clueless at the change in my wife. She was once such a homebody. I thought she liked cooking and taking care of all of us. I sense she is lying about a few things she does in her spare time.

Maybe I'm being paranoid after my little run in with some shady characters who hauled me off to some interrogation site. More details are in *Kifaru* if you're interested. Let me just say I was totally innocent. Anyway, it made me realize I needed to give Tessa a break and make this once in a while. Hope you enjoy it more than I do making it. If I ordered out it wouldn't get the appreciative kisses, I get for messing up the kitchen.

Ingredients

Stir Together:
1 c. warm water
1 yeast package
1 ½ c. all-purpose flour
Add To Mix:
1 whipped egg
1 T. vegetable oil
1 T. sugar
1 tsp. salt
Add:
2 c. more flour to mix.

Instructions

Knead for 5 minutes. Put in greased bowl and turn so all sizes are greased. Let rise for one hour. Punch down. Put in refrigerator for at least an hour. Roll out for use. Makes 2 doughs.

Perfect Piecrust (Martha Ervin)

I live next door to Tessa. I moved here when she was in Washington DC getting into all kinds of trouble. *Winds of Deception* can explain it better, I'm sure. My job at Enigma is caretaker for her children. I've done many jobs for them; some I don't talk about because it's classified. Those rascals have become my life and I would do anything to protect them. Anything. When Tessa goes on a mission, I fill in the gaps so their lives don't hit any potholes life can create. I keep this recipe on hand. They love to help me in the kitchen. Honestly, this helps me keep track of them. They are nonstop action.

Ingredients

Makes 5 piecrusts
4 c. unsifted all-purpose flour
1 T. sugar
2 tsp. salt
1 ¾ c. vegetable shortening
1 T. white or cider vinegar
1 large egg

Instructions

Mix first three ingredients well. Add shortening – mix until ingredients are crumbly.

In small bowl, beat together ½ c. water, vinegar, and egg. Combine both mixtures, stir until all ingredients are moistened. Divide dough in 5 portions. Roll out or store in refrigerator. Dough may be frozen or stored in refrigerator for 3 days.

Poppy Seed Bread (Martha Ervin)

3 c. all-purpose flour	1 ½ tsp. baking powder
2 ¼ c. sugar	1 ½ tsp. vanilla
3 eggs	1 ½ tsp. poppy seeds
1 ½ c. milk	1 ½ tsp. almond extract
1 1/8 c. oil	1 ½ tsp. butter flavoring
Glaze: ½ T. almond flavoring	**Glaze continued:**
¼ c. orange juice	½ T. vanilla
¼ c. powdered sugar	½ T. butter flavoring

Instructions

Mix all ingredients for bread, about 2 minutes. Pour into 2 lightly greased loaf pans. Bake 1 hour. Cool 3 or 4 minutes. Remove from pans. Punch with fork or toothpick. Pour the glaze over loaves. Can freeze if not used right away.

Entrées

Entree Actors

Agent Carter Johnson – He is a former NASA astronaut and came to Enigma after being kicked out of the space program. Known as a ladies' man, Carter got in trouble for dangling too many love affairs and ended up part of a murder conspiracy. Although brilliant, he doesn't have a serious bone in his body. Besides never seeing a mirror he didn't like, he can fly just about anything and isn't shy to share that information with you.

Roman Darya Petrov – The Enigma team first encountered this guy when they were in Afghanistan searching for Tessa who had gone missing in the high country. His reputation as a drug dealer, and shady arms dealer, did not endear him to Captain Chase Hunter, especially since he kidnapped Tessa. But it seems the man not only had a way with horses, but with Tessa's heart as well.

President Buck Austin – Besides being the most powerful man in the world, he is also the creator of Enigma. He calls on them when the other intelligence agencies and law enforcement need to keep their hands clean. He's a good old boy from Texas and just a little sweet on Tessa Scott for saving his life. He's not crazy about her husband and thinks he may just have to do something about that in the future.

Under Secretary of State Bonnie Finley – The woman feeds on powerful people and does whatever necessary to climb the ladder of success. Unfortunately, Tessa knows secrets concerning her personal life that might have that ladder come crashing down. Not to be out done, Bonnie also knows a thing or two about Tessa that could wreck her Little Miss Perfect image. Together they teamed up to survive Afghanistan and Russia in difficult circumstances.

Enigma Psychiatrist Dr. Wu – His job is to evaluate each agent after coming off a mission. Most of the team give him a hard time, especially Captain Hunter, by refusing to talk, share or take his suggestions as to avoiding things that could trigger their PTSD. Tessa Scott is a different story. She hangs on his every word and the two of them have become friends in spite of their perspective jobs. They share a love of gardening and he often uses this to reach in and rescue her from the dark side of the job.

Tessa Scott - You'd be surprised at what a wife and mother can do with a little imagination when confronted with a terrorist. Some heroes wear high heels and smell like chocolate chip cookies. Her name is Tessa. Here is a woman who believes spiders should be considered a terrorist threat and yet saved the president twice from an assassin. She came close to Captain Hunter killing her before she could explain why she was holding a gun on the president who was bleeding all over the floor. But it all worked out.

FBI Agent Dennis Martin – When Enigma was in Washington DC and the president got shot, Agent Martin was in hot water. Some felt like he somehow dropped the ball on some intel that could've been used to stop the chaos. It started a domino effect that could have made him lose his job and pension. Thanks to Captain Hunter, his mishaps were covered and the agent came out smelling like a rose. He would live to regret the obligation he now owes Enigma.

Chicken Dressing Casserole (Agent Carter Johnson)

I'm a Texan through and through. Why even President Buck Austin swings by to see me on the ranch when we're both within 100 miles of each other. His pretty little wife tries to keep him on a diet because of his cholesterol, but he doesn't have to worry about that when he comes to see me. He just doesn't bring her along. Now the Secret Service is another matter. They don't eat this kind of food because they'd be dropping like flies into a food coma. Can't have that.

Ingredients

Four Large boneless chicken breasts or more (about 4c.)
1 (10.5 oz.) can of cream of chicken soup
1 (10.5 oz.) can of mushroom soup
1 (8oz.) pkg. herb seasoned stuffing mix (one box never seems enough so I use half of a second box too.) And the cheap kind is just as good as the fancy kind.
½ c. butter, melted (Yes,s you can use margarine. Just don't tell me about it.)

Instructions

Cook chicken until tender. Remove from broth. Strain broth. Reserve 2 2/3 c. (I never get much broth so I just use a can of chicken broth. The whole can. Cut chicken into bite size pieces, set aside. This is where I'm going to go short cut for you. Combine all those ingredients in a 13x9x2 baking dish. Cover and refrigerate overnight. Remove casserole from refrigerator 30 minutes before baking. Uncover and bake 350 for 45-50 minutes.

My Beef Stroganoff (Roman Darya Petrov)
If you can't get a yak.

Yak meat is a sweet alternative to what is traditional red meat. Americans frown at this. It tastes a great deal like a buffalo/bison or elk, except it isn't gamey and never greasy. Since my mother was a Kyrgyz living in Northern Afghanistan and my father a Russian, I learned to adapt to cultural differences pretty quickly.

Ingredients & Instructions

Cut round steak or sirloin steak into strips. Put in bowl with flour, garlic, pepper (or whatever the heck you like in spices.) Coat the meat then brown it quickly. Doesn't have to be completely done.

Place in slow cooker with onions, mushrooms (usually I get fresh but this time I used a drained can of mushrooms and it was fine. Whatever you got.) Add the following:

One can of mushroom soup

Two cans beef broth (might only need one if you don't have a lot of meat. I always fix extra for a second or third meal. I freeze plates of it.)

Cook on low most of day or until it really looks done and tender. Before serving, add 1 small carton (again if there is a lot you might want more. I don't like sour cream, Tessa's kids do along with the man named Robert who lives with her.) Cook your egg noodles. Scoop meat over the top and you're done.

Baked Bean Casserole (Agent Carter Johnson – former astronaut) Texas Rocket Fuel

I'm here to tell you this is a man's meal. Serve it up with a side of biscuits and honey and you'll have your family full as a tick in summer. Goes great with all the barbeque meals too.

Ingredients

1 lb. cooked hamburger
8 pieces of cooked bacon crumbled
½ c. onions
2 T. of yellow mustard
½ c. of catsup

½ c. brown sugar
½ c. barbeque sauce (Optional. Take a chance)
3 cans baked beans

Instructions

If you don't like onions, you can leave them out, but honestly are you kidding me? Add the onions. You can also use 3 different kinds of beans if preferred. But seriously, are you going to ruin this with lima beans? I find that suspicious.

Combine and place in oven safe dish. Cook 1 hour at 350. Note: if the casserole looks a little dry then add more ketchup or barbeque sauce. It will be thick and hard to stir if needs more. You can also put this in a slow cooker on low if you have to run out for a while to save the world or pick up the kids from soccer practice or other events. Serve with slaw or salad and biscuits.

Cashew Chicken Recipe (Tierney James)

Ingredients

4 chicken breasts cut up in a bite size pieces

1 can chicken broth

1 can drained water chestnuts

1 tsp. ginger

1 tsp. garlic

1 tsp. pepper

¼ c. of soy sauce (I use more)

Chopped carrots, broccoli, onion, bell pepper

Cashews

Corn starch for thickening

Instructions

Stir fry chicken in cooking oil (olive or vegetable – I use both.) Remove. Stir fry vegetables. Only takes a couple of minutes. Leave a little crispness. Add chicken back in. Save about a ¼ of chicken broth and mix with cornstarch to make broth thick at the end. Add in drained water chestnuts. Then stir in ginger, garlic, pepper, soy sauce into broth. (you can go ahead and add the cornstarch mix if you can shake in a closed container so won't have lumps.) Stir into chicken vegetable mix. Cook until bubbly or hot through and through. Add cashews last minute or when you serve over rice. I have a container to mix my sauce so it won't be lumpy.

I double the chicken so I add more soy and more broth. If you feel at the end, it needs more broth, go ahead and add it. But you may need more thickening. I use a couple teaspoons of flour or cornstarch.

Lazy Chicken (Tierney James)

This is great to fix before you go to work in the morning. Then when you get home exhausted, stressed, cranky and don't want to cook, you'll open the frig and find this. One of the Enigma Team calls it Idiot Proof Chicken because it is so darn easy. Can you guess who said that? Such a diva

Ingredients

Four Chicken Breasts
Creamy Italian Dressing
Italian Bread Crumbs Preheat oven to 375.

Instructions

Preheat oven to 375.
Roll chicken in creamy Italian dressing then Italian Bread Crumbs.
Place in pan and cook for 45 minutes. (Check to see if done.)
Serve with wild rice and green beans.

Slow Cooker Fajitas (Tessa)

Ingredients

4 chicken breasts
1 sliced (or chopped) yellow onion
1 each sliced green, yellow, red pepper
1 can diced tomatoes with chilies
1 package fajita seasoning (sometimes I use taco if that's all I have)
Cherry or Roma tomatoes just in case you're stopped by the police.

Instructions

Layer half of onions and peppers. Put the chicken on top of veggies. Sprinkle the seasoning on top of chicken then add the remaining onions and peppers. Cook on high for four hours. Check chicken to see if cooked through. Sprinkle with salt, pepper and touch of garlic.

If it looks a little dry because you were late getting home due to being pulled over by the police for driving 60 in a 45-mph zone, add a few sliced cherry tomatoes or I use a Roma tomato if I have one. There had been a robbery at the nail salon. I mean really—who does that? Not my fault the escape vehicle in question looked like my SUV. Granted I did look like I was leaving the scene in a hurry. The officer wasn't amused when I started talking about chicken in the slow cooker at home. I think he thought I was being flippant.

Anyway, things like that make me slice or shred the chicken with a very sharp knife and fork while still in the cooker. Serve on warm tortillas. Toppings on the side: shredded cheese, sliced tomatoes, avocados, banana peppers, shredded lettuce. Of course, I include a big bottle of my favorite hot sauce. I also serve a spinach and fruit salad along with wild rice. It can easily serve a family of four. More people? More chicken. It is a very easy meal to prepare.

**Parmesan Garlic Chicken
(Undersecretary of State Bonnie Finley)**

Let me just say what an honor it is to be included in Tessa's little cookbook. She and I have our differences, but we both decided to keep each other's secrets when we got stuck in Afghanistan. I owe her a great debt because of her sacrifice with that notorious Kyrgyz tribesman called Darya in order to save our skins. I will say no more about that. What I can say is the woman is no chicken when it comes to protecting orphan girls.

Ingredients

½ tsp. garlic powder
6 boneless skinless chicken breast halves (2 lbs.)
½ c. grated parmesan cheese
1 envelope Italian salad dressing mix

Instructions

Mix cheese, garlic powder, salad dressing mix. Moisten chicken with water then coat with cheese mixture. Place in shallow baking dish. Bake at 400 degrees for about 30 minutes or until chicken is cooked through.

Mexican Chicken (Tessa)

Ingredients

1 cooked & boned chicken
1 can cream of mushroom soup
1 can cream of chicken soup
1 c. chicken broth
Red cayenne pepper
½ can Rotel
1 bag Doritos
½ medium chopped onion
½ lb. Velveeta sliced cheese

Instructions

Place chicken in a 9 x 13 pan. Sprinkle with pepper. Add the onion and sliced cheese. Combine the soups, broth and Rotels. Pour half over the chicken Add the crushed Doritos. Pour remaining mixture on the Doritos and repeat. Bake at 400 degrees for 30 minutes and serve with more chips.

Pepper Steak (President Buck Austin)

Well, I don't get to cook much now that there is a full-time kitchen staff to make whatever I want. But since Tessa wanted me to submit something for this project, this is what I came up with. I mean, I owe her big time for saving my life. (*Winds of Deception*) Nothing like getting shot during a hurricane by a bunch of misfits. I can laugh about it now. To think that little gal stood up to them, still just impresses the heck out of me.

Ingredients

3 c. cooked rice	1 c. sliced green onion
1 lb. round steak	2 chopped green bell peppers
1 T. paprika	2 T. cornstarch
1 tsp. butter	¼ c. soy sauce
2 clove garlic	2 fresh tomatoes
1 can beef broth	¼ c. water

Instructions

Pound steak into ¼ inch thickness. Sprinkle with paprika. Brown meat in the butter. Add garlic and broth. Cover and simmer 30 minutes. Stir in onions and green bell peppers. Cover and cook five minutes. Blend in the cornstarch, soy sauce and water. Cook about two minutes. Add tomatoes and cook until hot and bubbly. Serve over cooked white rice.

Shrimp Remoulade (Dr. Wu - Enigma physiatrist)

I'm kind of offended that the other agents thought I should submit a Chinese recipe just because of my heritage. I don't even like Chinese food. I like Cajun food. I went to a university in Louisiana to get my degree in medicine. As a matter of fact, I learned a great deal from Madame Lacreasa, a fine voodoo advisor in her own right. This is probably why Captain Hunter doesn't trust me and thinks I'm a mind bender. That and I have an image of him on a doll next to my bed where I keep a small bowl of sharp pins.

Ingredients

½ c. chopped green onions	½ c. Bavarian style mustard
¼ c. chopped green bell pepper	½ tsp. garlic
¼ c. chopped parsley	1 tsp. salt
½ c. hardboiled egg chopped	¼ tsp. red pepper or Tabasco
2 c. mayonnaise	3 lbs. of shrimp

Instructions

Remove shell and veins for the raw shrimp, then cook in a little water until pink (5-10 minutes) I hate this step so I buy the frozen. I know that sounds a little lazy but it is what it is.

Remoulade Dressing:

Place onions, parsley, green pepper in a blender with hardboiled egg. Mayonnaise and mustard are added along with seasonings. Mixture is blended until thick and smooth.

Assemble the plates with shredded lettuce to form a base for the shrimp. The Remoulade Dressing is spooned generously over the shrimp. Place a bowl of the dressing on the side for anyone who wants more. Fresh asparagus spears, cocktail tomatoes and a hot roll complete your luncheon or dinner.

Make My Day, You Chicken (FBI Agent Martin)

Because I live alone, I can eat on this a couple of days. However, I did make it at Tessa's house one Christmas for the crowd she seems to accumulate. It didn't last long. Those kids of hers are the reason third world countries are starving. They'd eat the table legs if they weren't attached. I know Tessa and her sketchy friends and I don't always see eye to eye, but they managed to give me a thumbs up after eating my delicately prepared dish. High praise coming from the mighty Captain Hunter (like I care if he eats it).

Ingredients

4-5 large chicken breasts cut into strips
Slice one small onion
Peel and slice one zucchini
Cut a bell pepper into strips
Taco seasoning

Instructions

Place ingredients in bowl and coat with olive oil. Spread contents onto a cookie sheet. Cook at 500 degrees for 15-20 minutes. Good with rice or use warm tortillas. Add a salad and you got a meal.

SOUPS & SALADS

Soup & Salad Actors

Tessa Scott's Life That Flipped Her Into Seeking Adventure

Oh my gosh! Robert and I went to the hardware store today to buy a few things for our remodeled powder room. You would think we were in some kind of reality show or decorating contest for as long as it took. I say get what you like, looks good and fits your style. He over analyzes each screw, bolt, beveled verses flat item on the list. Of course, if he can get it cheaper at the Habitat Store for pennies (no matter if it's dented or dinged) then that makes much more sense. He does make sure I'm okay with the choice. Most of the time, I am. After the marathon selection process, we headed home.

I couldn't help but wonder if Chase would even care what kind of mirror I chose. Would he shrug with a slow irritation that I even asked his opinion? The man has a black and white apartment that looks like it arrived in a box from some online store. No pictures or mementos sitting around. Just a violin propped in the corner he claims to know how to play and some old books that smells like the inside of a musty flea market. Unlike Robert, he believes life is a series of rooms all done in black and white. I've thought about sneaking in someday and stencil the words, "Keep it simple, stupid" over the fireplace.

Back to Robert. He's a good man. Not very romantic, but definitely a good guy. At least once a week one of my girlfriends tells me how lucky I am to have him. I smile and nod. They've never been to a big box store with him to buy paint. Our idea of chic or urban country style differs enough that ends in the silent treatment on the ride home. Then I just go buy what I want. The last time I painted he never acknowledged the change until someone showed interest. Believe it or not he said: "I told Tessa to just get whatever she thought best. I trust her completely."

Probably wouldn't say that if he knew I live a secret life working with a nondescript government agency. Does that sound like someone you can trust? Wonder what he'd think knowing I decided to work for Enigma because I have this over powering need to be thrilled. Paint colors, new bathroom fixtures and salvaged do-dads from the resale store doesn't do it for me. Knowing I make a difference in the lives of those who protect this country, from monsters of terror, keeps my heart beating at a rate that can't be considered healthy. I say it's the work. Sometimes I think it's something else.

Isn't life kind of like a soup or salad most days? Think about your choices when you make these and wonder why that internet truck is parked outside your house from a company you've never heard of. Probably Enigma checking up on you since you're reading this book. Just go the door and wave. Messes with their head every time. LOL

Captain Chase Hunter - He believed watching Tessa Scott's children for one night would be an easy assignment. What he hadn't considered was how much they resembled miniature, domestic terrorists. The former Delta Force officer discovers, outmaneuvering the Taliban was child's play compared to keeping three kids from falling victim to a group of not-so-smart burglars. But with their flare for the dramatic and enough plastic firepower to make Darth Vader tremble, the children give him memories he'll never forget.

Agent Samantha Cordova – She has a relationship with the Prime Minister of Israel and yes, he is Director Benjamin Clark's half-brother. No conflict of interest since she is faithful in telling each man what the other one may or may not be up to. The director thinks it's a win, win situation. Agent Carter Johnson doesn't like it much so he plays hard to get when she's around. The trouble is she may just destroy him if he isn't careful with that attitude.

Agent Nicholas Zoric – Known as The Vampire in some circles because he enjoys his job of interrogator a little too much. Strange that he is terrified of snakes.

Agent Vernon Kemp – Secretly in love with Agent Samantha Cordova, he can barely speak when she's in the room. To her credit, Sam is kind to him but still manages to tease him with bending down and whispering sweet words in his ear. He's been known to spill coffee on his keyboard during such incidents.

Martha & Francis Ervin – This husband-and-wife team give Tessa a sense of extended family. Francis works as a Biblical archeologist which gets him and the others in and out of the Middle East from time to time. Francis first met Tessa on his way to Washington DC. The rest is history as they say.

No Fail Potato Soup (Tessa)
Lifesaver soup when you need one.

Ingredients

1 c. chopped celery
1 c. chopped onion
Half stick of butter
Place ingredients in bowl then microwave for five minutes. Afterwards combine with the following.
One can drained chopped potatoes. (If I'm not in a hurry then I cook them fresh before adding them to the mixture.)
5-6 cans of Cream of Potato Soup
1 quart Half & Half
I use the slow cooker on low so I can go about my day. Just before serving I add one fourth cup of instant mashed potatoes. (More if you like it thicker.) You can have toppings like chopped green onions, shredded cheese and bacon bits.

Homemade Keto Chili (Capt. Chase Hunter)
Because the world can be a cold place.

I don't generally cook. Most of the time I fix something I can eat over the sink. Makes cleanup easier and it's very efficient. But when there's going to be a strategy meeting on an upcoming mission at the Warehouse that usually last most of the day and into the night, this comes in real handy. Since we have a kitchen at the Warehouse, I tell Gunny Segreant Tom Cooper and Lieutenant Ken Montgomery to have all the ingredients except the meat. I bring that. With any luck, Tessa will bring something sweet.

Ingredients

3 lbs. ground beef (uncooked)	½ onion, chopped
1 cup celery, diced	2 (8 oz.) cans tomato sauce
14.5 oz can stew tomatoes	14.5 oz can fire roasted diced tomato
1 tsp chili powder	2 tsp sea salt
2 tsp garlic powder	1 tsp onion powder
½ tsp black pepper	1 bay leaf
1 cup chopped bell pepper (any color)	Add a few diced garden tomatoes if available

Instructions

Add all ingredients into a slow cooker. Cook on low 6-8 hours.

Notes

Beef can be started from frozen. Break beef up after cooking 1-2 hrs. Plan to cook for a total of 8 hours.

Clam Chowder (Nicholas Zoric)

Sauté an onion, celery and stick of butter in microwave for five minutes.

Add the above to the following in a slow cooker.

3 Cans Campbells Clam Chowder Soup

2 Cans Campbell's Potato Soup

1 quart Half and Half

1 (6 ounce) can of minced clams

Cook on low for four hours. Stir several times to keep from sticking.

Homemade Chicken Noodle Soup (Tessa)

Ingredients

It's better with homemade chicken stock but I don't always have that.

½cup diced carrots

¼ cup diced onion

1-2 stalks of diced celery.

Toss all that in the pot with a tablespoon of butter and sauté until it starts to get tinder. Add in 6 cups of chicken broth or stock. Then the dry ingredients:

1 tsp (or less) of salt,

½ tsp black pepper,

½ tsp (maybe a bit more) thyme,

1 tablespoon of dried (or fresh) parsley.

While that's coming back up to boil, I open a can of chicken, drain, and chop it up a bit finer on the cutting board, then add to soup. I'll let it low boil for about 10-15 minutes to make sure the veggies are soft.

Add in 1 1/4 cups of egg noodles and cook until they're tender and you're ready to eat. I've frozen it before but when I know I'm going to do that I don't add the noodles. I'll wait to add them after it's thawed out and heating up.

Angry Mandarin Salad (Tessa)

I like to serve this when I make the cashew chicken recipe in the main course section. It is a touch of sweet for such a meal. It's also pretty to look at. I find that the kids are more likely to eat it and especially a person who is picky about eating vegetables. I once made this for a bridesmaid's brunch. I added some pieces of grilled chicken and served with poppyseed dressing. Individual bowls or one large clear glass serving dish will make this salad to die for.

Ingredients:

Ripped lettuce, spinach & romaine	Blueberries
Slice strawberries	Fresh Parmesan Cheese
1 can Mandarin oranges drained	Chopped pecans
Chopped celery	Chicken added for a main dish

Instructions

Combine all the above ingredients except pecans and cheese. Before serving add the fresh parmesan cheese and pieces of pecans. Poppyseed dressing is my favorite, but half the time I use nothing at all.

I usually make individual plates for each of my family or guests. It's prettier and actually makes my kids want to eat. The other option is a buffet style where I have all the ingredients in clear bowls and people make their own. Not everyone likes nuts or celery. Go figure! Then if there are leftovers it's quick and easy clean up and can be served the next day because you're sick and tired of feeding everyone. That's why I call it Angry Mandarin Salad. You can call it whatever you like.

NOTES

Homemade Hummus (Samantha Cordova)

Unlike Tessa and her little family of misbehaved trouble makers, I serve things that are healthy and easy to digest, especially if you are saving the world on a daily basis. I don't have time for all that individual serving nonsense. I mean if they can't get their own plate or contribute to the meal, they've come to the wrong house. If you want to be served then go to a restaurant. I'm busy. But I do love this hummus and it lasts for a week in an airtight container. When I go to Israel to visit Prime Minister Levi Gilad, he loves for me to make it for him. He's always very appreciative, I might add.

Ingredients:

1 (15 oz.) can of chickpeas
¼ c. well-stirred tahini
½ tsp. ground cumin
2 T. extra-virgin olive oil, more for the serving
1-3 T. water

¼ c. lemon juice
1 small garlic clove, minced
Salt to taste
A dash of ground paprika for the serving

Instructions:

Using a food processor, combine the tahini and lemon juice and process for 1 minute. Scrape the sides, as well as the bottom then process for 30 more seconds. This will "whip" (one of my favorite words) the tahini, making the hummus smooth, even creamy.

Add the olive oil, garlic, cumin and a ½ teaspoon of salt to the tahini and lemon juice. Process 30 more seconds, then scrape inside the bowl for a second time. Process for another 30 seconds to make sure it is well blended.

Open, drain, rinse the chickpeas. Add half the chickpeas to the food processor and process for 1 minute. Scrape again then add the remaining chickpeas. Process until thick and smooth, 1-2 minutes.

You'll think the hummus is too thick and notice there are still pieces of chickpea. Since I hate that I find if I add 2-3 Tbsp of water and process slowly, I can reach perfection. You know, just like me.

Taste for salt and adjust as needed. (I don't like a lot but obviously Tessa does since she always looks like she's retaining water.) Serve hummus with a drizzle of olive oil and a dash of paprika. Store in airtight container and refrigerate up to one week.

●────────────────────────●

Sweet Pasta Salad (Tessa)

16-ounce Rotini noodles, cooked and drained
Add ½ c. olive oil (I've used canola oil too)
Mix:

½ c. white vinegar	1 onion chopped fine
1 ½ c. sugar	1 tsp. salt
1 T. mustard	1 T. garlic powder
1 cucumber peeled & shredded	1 T parsley

Add mixture to noodles. Refrigerate overnight. Shredded cheese is a nice add in if desired.

Barbarian Pasta Salad or Choke Arti (Nicholas Zoric)

Needless to say, I really get off on making this pasta salad because it has so many words that describe what I do for the Enigma team. When Tessa makes this, she leaves out the artichokes because she doesn't like them. But her kids always ask when they see her fixing a pasta salad. 'Are we going to choke Arti tonight?' For some reason she doesn't find it nearly as amusing as I do.

Ingredients

4 oz. uncooked spaghetti noodles
1 (6 oz.) marinated artichokes
¼ c. sliced fresh zucchini
2/3 c. shredded carrots
2 oz. sliced salami cut in strips
4 oz (1 c.) shredded mozzarella cheese
2 T. vegetable oil
½ tsp. dried whole basil
1 clove garlic crushed
2 T. vinegar
¾ tsp. dry mustard
½ tsp. dried whole or
2 T. parmesan cheese

Instructions

Break spaghetti noodles in pieces then cook according to your directions. Drain noodles when fully cooked. Drain the artichokes but save the juice. Chop artichokes. Combine all ingredients except the spices and oil. Combine the liquid and spices in a jar. Cover. Shake. Pour over spaghetti. Cover and chill. 6-8 servings.

Absolutely No Vitamins Broccoli Raisin Salad (Tessa)

I'm ashamed to admit, I deceive my family by telling them this is not nutritious and to only eat a teaspoon full. Of course, it is full of vitamins, especially iron, and I pretend to withhold it so they'll like it better. I fuss a bit when they ask for more and pretend not to be sure it's the right thing to do. Boy, could I tell you stories! But with a little begging, I load them up with my salad. Now if you don't like mayonnaise, you might try it with a ranch style dressing. I have extra bacon, just in case war breaks out at the table. Whatever it takes, right?

Ingredients

Make the dressing in a large bowl
1 c. mayonnaise
½ c. sugar
1 ½ tbsp. vinegar
After you've made the dressing add:
6 c. broccoli florets
1 small diced onion
1 c. raisins
Put the broccoli bowl in the refrigerator for a couple hours so the flavors will mingle. When ready to serve add:
10 strips of crumbled fried bacon
¾ c sunflower seeds

Orange-Cream Fruit Salad (Tessa)

Ingredients

1 (20 oz.) can pineapple tidbits, drained

1 (11 oz.) can mandarin oranges, drained

2 apples, cored and chopped

1 (3 3/4 – or 3 5/8 oz. pkg.) instant vanilla pudding mix

½ of 6 oz. can (1/3 c.) frozen orange juice Concentrate - thawed

¾ c. sour cream

1 (16 oz.) can peach slices, drained

3 medium bananas, sliced

1 ½ c. milk

Lettuce cups

Instructions

In a bowl, combine fruits, set aside. In small bowl combine dry pudding, milk, and orange juice. Beat with a rotary beater, until blended, 1-2 minutes. Beat in the sour cream. Fold into the fruit mix. Cover and chill. Makes 10 servings.

Strawberry Fluff Salad (Tessa)

This is a great dish to take to your church potluck or in my case when the team comes over to my secret apartment and I don't have a lot of time to cook. The look of pure joy on their faces reminds me of when they take out a terrorist. Oh wait. Did I really say that? I mean when it snows at Christmas.

Ingredients

1 small box of strawberry gelatin

1 large can crush pineapple, drained

1 c. hot water

½ c. cold water

½ c. pineapple juice

1 c. chopped pecans

1 large contained of frozen whipped topping

8 oz. pkg. cream cheese

½ c. sugar

Instructions

Prepare gelatin with hot and cold water plus the pineapple juice. Let partially set in refrigerator. Mix sugar and cream cheese with pecans, and whipped topping. Add to gelatin mixture and let set in refrigerator.

Fruit & Nut Tropical Slaw (Vernon Kemp)

I confess that I don't really make this myself. One of the computer techs who has a crush on me makes it for me. She offered to show me how, but that seemed like a big step on the road to commitment. I can barely talk to Samantha without slipping in my own drool. Instead, I got a copy of the recipe from the tech. Tessa makes it for me to bring to get togethers at her secret apartment in Sacramento near the university campus. She keeps my little secret.

Ingredients

1 (8 ¼ oz.) can pineapple slices	1 (11 oz.) can Mandarin orange sections drained
1 T. lemon juice	½ c. chopped walnuts
1 medium banana sliced	¼ c. raisins
3 c. shredded cabbage	1 (8 oz.) carton orange yogurt
1 c. thinly sliced celery	½ tsp. salt

Instructions

Drain pineapple (reserve 2 T. syrup) Cut up pineapple: set aside. Combine the reserve syrup and lemon juice. Coat banana slices with 1 T. of the juice mixture then set remaining juice aside. In a large bowl combine pineapple, banana, cabbage, celery, oranges, nuts and raisins. Blend the reserved juice mixture with the yogurt and salt. Add to the cabbage mixture then toss lightly to coat. Cover and chill. Makes 8-10 servings.

The Ervin Cranberry Sauce (Marth & Francis Ervin)

Ingredients

    1 pkg. whole cranberries
    1 c. brown sugar
    1 c. water
    1 orange or tangelo
    Apple pie spice

Instructions

In a medium sauce pan, add cranberries, brown sugar and water. Squeeze the juice of the orange or tangelo into the pan. Add a dash of apple pie spice. Bring to a boil and then reduce heat (do not let boil) for ten minutes, stirring often. Put it in a bowl to cool. The brown sugar takes the bitterness away, giving the cranberry sauce a warm feeling. I have used this for years. I hope you enjoy it.

WHOSE SIDE ARE YOU ON ANYWAY
Vegetable Sides & Other Nonsense

Tessa's Introduction to Captain Hunter

Captain Chase Hunter is a no-nonsense, ex-Delta Force, captain. He stampedes around my life like a F5 tornado. With a chip on his shoulder and anger management issues, it's a wonder the president even wanted him to be a team leader at Enigma. I guess when you save the president's life, his way of thanking you is to put you in even more danger. I know this because I had the misfortune of giving him over three pints of my blood once. Not exactly my best day! Next thing I knew, I was working for Enigma.

Anyway, back to the captain. He's over six foot with a definite Cherokee heritage showing in those high cheek bones and dark skin. He's not a handsome man but holy cow, he certainly takes my breath away with those chocolate brown eyes and wide mouth. Did I mention he's as strong as an ox with ... Goodness. I think I'm going to have to go splash some water on my face. Let's just skip the description.

We get along most of the time. I probably talk to him more than my husband about the kids, world events and my dreams. What always amazes me is that he actually listens to me. It's a little disturbing at times because he seems to hold his breath at every word. A number of times he's told me I'm the only person who can make him laugh. One thing that concerns me is he rubs a spot on his chest when I'm around. It's like I'm the reason he's in pain. The others on the team have never noticed it. Only me. Robert only listens to me if food or sex is involved.

And no, I'm not sleeping with the captain. Well, there was that one time when we first met. It was really very innocent, at least on my part. We were on a mission, one king size bed and he being the gentleman, slept on the floor. I promise I didn't know he'd get off the floor during the night, turn up the air and crawl into bed when I was sound asleep. Somehow the cold made me gravitate into his arms. Nothing happened. Horrified, I set some kind of record jumping out of the bed the next morning. I didn't think he would ever stop laughing. Even today, he holds that over my head.

So why did I share a room with him in the first place? I didn't have a choice. He didn't trust me because I sort of tried to escape several times. Totally not my fault. Robert had taken the children on a trip to Tahoe so it was out of the question I call for help. After all, I was being watched by some crack pot agency at Homeland Security. I should have been safe. Right?

Those days started me on a journey that changed everything. The only person who knows the truth about me is Tierney James. If Enigma finds out about her she could be in danger too. She'd probably love working for them. At this point I'm just trying to keep my head above water with these guys. Every time I plan to quit, Chase does something that makes me realize I never will.

Sometimes I think I'm falling in love with him.

Whose Side Are You on Anyway Actors

Director Benjamin Clark – The job of the director is to manage all the Enigma teams at the twelve universities in which they are located. We see him working with the Sacramento team that takes the lead on every operation. He is former military and thinks of Captain Hunter as a son he never had. He's tough, doesn't like change, and refuses to accept defiance among his people. One of the things that he hates the most is the way Vernon Kemp dresses like a beach bum.

FBI Agent Dennis Martin – This agent fades in and out of the Enigma series because he also works for the FBI. It comes in useful to have someone on the inside that can get the Enigma team what they want ASAP. He doesn't like any of the agents, especially Tessa, who he believes is pulling all the strings with her sweet attitude and optimistic outlook on life. It's hard to be snarky with her when she calls him an old softy.

Vernon Kemp – Shy around the females at Enigma, he finds other ways to impress them, like hacking into the Pentagon and NORAD. That hasn't always gone like he planned.

Army Ranger Lieutenant Ken Montgomery – Serving with Captain Hunter in Afghanistan gave him a hard-core outlook on life and how things need to change. Able to step up in a moment's notice to take charge, the two men have become close friends. He's most at home on the battlefield.

Gunny Sergeant Tom Cooper – Some call him a silent giant given he's six foot five and built like a tank. He's more of an acute observer than someone who participates in social conversation. No one at Enigma presses him to change. His devotion to country and his teammates are beyond reproach.

Nicholas Zoric – An accomplished artist, his work is displayed all over the world. His specialty is creating heavenly scenes that involves angels interacting with humans. This is a cover for his Enigma job which is acting as interrogator. Being a heavy smoker, Serbian and looking like Count Dracula gives him a very intimidating aura that scares most people before he ever gets started.

Broccoli Rice Casserole (Director Benjamin Clark)

I like things efficient and streamlined. This recipe combines a lot of things to feed everyone without having to make a lot of side dishes no one will eat. You can make it ahead, which as far as I'm concerned, is strategic planning. That's all I'm going to say on the matter, except if you use margarine instead of butter you deserve to be court martialed. And I'll see to it.

Ingredients

1 pkg. frozen chopped broccoli	1 can mushroom soup
1 medium onion chopped	2 c. Minute Rice
1 c. chopped celery	1 small jar of cheese
1 stick butter	Salt to taste

Instructions

Cook broccoli according to package directions. Drain. Sauté onion and celery in butter. Combine all ingredients. Mix well. Turn into a well-greased casserole dish. Bake at 350 degrees for 20-30 minutes. Serve hot. Should be enough for twelve people unless you're feeding my men and Tessa's kids. In that scenario—good luck.

Corn Casserole (Vernon Kemp)

This is another idiot proof recipe according to Samantha, so she let me use it. I'm not sure what she means by that since I'm clearly the smartest one at Enigma.

Ingredients

1 can cream corn
1 can regular corn, drained
1 box Jiffy Cornbread Mix
8 oz. carton of sour cream
1 stick melted butter

Instructions

Mix together the ingredients and place in an 8 x 8 oven dish. Bake at 350 degrees for 45 minutes. Sometimes I add a tablespoon or two of sugar to the mix. If Tessa knew this, she'd have me kicked out of Enigma. In her Tennessee head, sugar mixed with cornbread is a recipe for Satan spawn.

Funeral Potatoes
(Army Ranger Lieutenant Ken Montgomery)

Easy recipe to make for that special occasion, like a funeral and you don't want to go empty handed. Does that sound right? Makes a lot and can put those rowdy guests straight into a food coma. This all sounds way inappropriate and I'm sure Tessa will feel a lecture coming on when she sees this. Did I mention she saved my life the first day we met? (*An Unlikely Hero*) That's why I give her some slack at trying to tell me the ins and outs of funeral etiquette. Anyway, make it, eat it. It's good.

Ingredients

20 oz bag of hash browns (thaw one hour)
½ c. melted butter
2 small cartons sour cream

2 c. crushed corn flakes + ¼ c. melted butter
1 can mushroom soup
1 ½ c. grated cheddar cheese

Instructions

Combine all the ingredients then top with corn flakes and ¼ c. melted butter in a 9 x 13 dish. Bake at 350 degrees for 40-50 minutes.

Never Go Back Potatoes (Tierney James)

Crazy name, right? After you make these easy potatoes and your family won't eat anything else from then on, you'll never go back to whatever you were doing before.

Ingredients

2-3 lbs. diced potatoes in bowl
Olive Oil
Garlic, Parsley, Salt, Pepper, Onion Powder

Instructions

Pour olive oil over the raw potatoes and coat. Then spoon them onto a cookie sheet big enough to hold the potatoes without layering them too much. It's okay to spoon more olive oil over them from the bowl. Sprinkle the herbs on top. Place in 400 degrees oven for 50 minutes. If not tender add a little more time. I cook only about 45 minutes because I don't want them completely done. I then put them in a slow cooker on low to finish up to have later. These can be made ahead if you're going to use the slow cooker.

Apple Mallow Sweet Potatoes (Tierney James)

Ingredients

2 apples sliced
1/3 c. chopped pecans
½ c. packed brown sugar
½ tsp. cinnamon

2 (17 oz.s) cans yams drained
¼ c. butter
2 c. marshmallows

Instructions

Toss apples and nuts with combined brown sugar and cinnamon. Alternate layers of apples and yams in 1 ½ quart casserole dish. Dot with the butter. Cover. Bake at 350 degrees for 35-40 minutes. Sprinkle marshmallows over the yams and apples. Broil until lightly brown. 6-8 servings unless you have people who think they're eating for two.

Deviled Eggs (Nicholas Zoric)

Boil 6-10 eggs until hard boiled. Remove shells, slice open (my favorite part) and let cool. Spoon out the yokes into a bowl and mix in Durkee Famous Sandwich Sauce instead of mayonnaise. Replace mixture back into the egg white. Sprinkle with paprika. You can also use hot pepper flakes and bacon bits on some of the eggs.

Cheese Bites (Gunny Sergeant Tom Cooper)

People think because I'm built like a brick wall and believe that conversation is not only unnecessary, but is a waste of oxygen, that I am without any social graces or gifts. It might surprise you that I enjoy cooking. That hasn't always been the case. After Tessa caused me to have a concussion using nothing but a broomstick, I woke up in the hospital, watching cooking shows. I aspire to have my own someday. This next recipe is an appetizer.

Ingredients

1 ½ lbs. Monterey Jack Cheese
¾ lb. of Cheddar
3 eggs
¼ c. milk
1 T. All-purpose flour
2 (4 oz.) cans chopped green chilies

Instructions

Grate the cheese and combine. Grease a 9 x 13 dish. Spread half of the cheese in the dish then place the chilies on the cheese. Add the rest of the cheese. Beat eggs, milk, and flour. Pour evenly over the contents. Bake at 350 degrees for 40-45 minutes. Should be lightly browned. Let stand 3-5 minutes. Then cut into small squares. You can also add some chopped onions and bell peppers if you don't like chilies.

Cheese Ball (FBI Agent Dennis Martin)

Even the name sounds like a new kind of sport for those who like to stand around and snack in front of a bunch of strangers. I don't like crowds because I'm always trying to decide who is the liar in the bunch. But Tessa says I need to chill out and I'll have to admit, this is a tasty side if you're late getting dinner on the table. Hope Tessa is getting the hint here.

Instructions

1 (8 oz.) pkg. cream cheese	1 T. Worcestershire Sauce
1 cheese ball from dairy section of store	1 T. green pepper
1 T. chopped pimento	1 T. lemon juice
1 T. chopped onion	1 T. margarine

Instructions

Soften the cheese and cream cheese. Mix all together with mixer. Shape into ball and chill. Serve with celery, crackers and toasted French bread.

NOTES

JUST DESERTS

The Tessa Story Continues

Laundry piles up when I work, act as chauffeur, try to keep meals on the table and volunteer at the food pantry for my church. There are dust bunnies under my kid's bed that look like ostrich eggs. The other day Daniel went to get his soccer ball and brought one of those to the car instead. I was not amused. Then my husband, Robert said I needed to cut something out to make more time for the house. After all I was the one that wanted a bigger house. If I couldn't take care of it maybe we should downsize.

Have you ever had that moment when you see Rambo's body but your head is where Sylvester's Stallone's should be? Then you lift your machine gun in the air and start firing, while screaming your outrage because the toilet overflowed? Me too! So, I pop the Totally Zen CD into the car thingy and crank that puppy up on high, hoping to outlast the "Let It Go" song from Frozen my daughter is singing in the back seat while her brothers practice their Kung Fu on each other.

When I was captured by this guy named Amon from Egypt, he kept telling me not to be afraid. I nearly became hysterical with laughter. I told him I had three kids and taught in a public junior high school. "Not much scares me," I snorted. Yeah. I snorted. Not very dignified, but I'd just been kidnapped and thrown in the floor board of a car. The driver thought he was Mario Andretti or something the way he kept swerving and gunning the engine. I guess he thought he could outrun the hurricane that was over us. Idiot.

Oh! My point! Being a mom and housewife gets a little dicey at times. You can't always be Martha Stewart for the Roberts of this world. Find something to relieve the stress; hot bubble bath, spa day or for me it's working at Enigma fighting terrorists. Robert doesn't even know I keep a gun Velcroed to the top inside drawer of the nightstand. Sometimes secrets are a good thing.

Just Dessert Actors

Tessa Scott – Tessa sometimes follows her heart inside of her brain. When her friend, Handsome Jones needs her help, she finds herself in the crosshairs of a corrupt dictator. She convinces the Enigma team of the worthy cause and nearly loses her life.

Honey Lynch – This Irish Assassin is not a member of the Enigma team. She plays both sides against the middle and usually decides to help the good guys. Dangerous and a bit psycho, Honey has decided to make Tessa her new best friend. The chocolate chip cookie baking mom is terrified to tell her it isn't true. However, they make a nice and often, humorous team.

Agent Samantha Cordova – When Sam, as the team call her, isn't saving the world, she is thinking of clever ways to get rid of Tessa. Once she was put in charge of training her nemesis, she focused on daily abuse rather than end of life scenarios. Secretly, the two have begun trying to be friends. But like a forest fire, sometimes their hatred of each other just flares up and Captain Hunter has to put out the fire.

Secret Service Agent Willy Robbins – The agent has proved herself to be a possible new agent for Enigma. She started out as a school counselor, went on to get her master's degree in profiling and a Ph.D. in criminal law. She then joined the Secret Service. She came to the attention of Director Benjamin Clark after helping with protecting the future king of Saudi Arabia. There is more on her in the book *Martyrs Never Die.*

Sean Patrick Scott – This is Tessa's oldest and most devious child who plans to conquer the world after graduating from West Point. He gets into all kinds of mischief, but always come out on top. Captain Hunter keeps an eye on him because the the kid reminds him of his younger self.

Daniel Scott – Being the middle child has its disadvantages, but Daniel makes the most of everything he comes across. He is gifted in electronics and is being tutored in computer science by none other than Vernon Kemp. What could go wrong there?

Heather Scott – She wants to grow up and be a real-life princess who rides a unicorn. In the meantime, she is slowly wrapping Captain Hunter around her little finger. Besides being a great deal like her mother, Heather has learned that the way to a man's heart is through his stomach. Therefore, the captain and the other men will eat anything the little monster puts in front of them.

Tessa's story continues: This first recipe is part of the reason Enigma has kept me around so long. They love my chocolate chip cookies. Even the crown prince of Saudi Arabia loves them. Well, that's what he said the day after I saved his life from a group of assassins. Maybe he appreciated me getting my new clothes all bloody and ripped on his behalf. You can read all about that in *Martyrs Never Die* if you want the whole story. In the meantime, try these easy cookies. I included an alternative one you can make with oatmeal which is also excellent.

The Real Deal Enigma Chocolate Chip Cookies (Tessa)

Ingredients & Instructions

Preheat oven to 375 degrees
In a bowl mix:
2 sticks of softened butter (If you use margarine, you are dead to me!)
2 eggs
1 tsp. vanilla (Do you see flavoring here? Of course not! Don't be ridiculous.)
1 c. brown sugar
1 c. granulated sugar
1 tsp. baking soda
Gradually add:
3 c. all-purpose flour
1 (11.5 oz.) bag of Ghirardelli Milk Chocolates (You can use other brands. This is my favorite.)
¾ c. chopped pecans (optional)
Bake 9-10 minutes. Cool. Makes 4 dozen.

Chocolate Chip Oatmeal Cookies (Tessa)

Ingredients

2 sticks butter
1 c. sugar
1 c. brown sugar
2 eggs
1 tsp. vanilla
2 c. All-purpose flour

2 ½ c. quick cook oats
½ tsp. salt
1 tsp. baking powder
1 tsp. baking soda
1 c. chopped pecans
12 oz. bag of milk chocolate chips

Instructions

In a large mixing bowl (better to use stand mixer as batter is very thick) cream together butter and sugars. Add the eggs mixing in one at a time. Add vanilla. Beat till smooth. In another bowl combine oats, flour, salt, baking powder. Mix dry ingredients with wet ingredients. Stir in chocolate chips and pecans. Bake at 350 for 9-11 minutes. Do not over-bake. Cookies will harden as they cool.

Fruit Freezes (Tessa)

1 (20 oz.) can crushed pineapple with juice
3 bananas chopped
Several cups of your favorite fruit chopped or use one can of fruit cocktail drained
Half cup of orange juice (sometimes I use grape juice)
Marchino sliced cherries, drained
Mix in large bowl. Place in one cup containers. Add three or four cherries to each one. Freeze.

When I serve these, I put several in the microwave and nuke for 30 seconds to make them a little slushie to eat. Really good over cottage cheese too. Kids think they're getting a special treat.

No Fail Cheesecake – Because life is complicated enough (Tessa)

I'm a working mom. Easy is my love language.

Ingredients

1 graham cracker crust
Combine:
1 bar of cream cheese softened
1 can of condensed milk
1/3 c. of lemon juice
1 tsp. vanilla

Instructions

Blend with mixer and pour into crust. Chill. Can top with your favorite fruit or sauce. Canned pie filling works great. Carmel or chocolate sauce is also a good choice. Pick your weakness. It's only cheesecake.

Left Over Cake Dessert (Tessa)

(When your life has gotten a little stale. Cake! Seriously, I mean cake.)

Pinch up cake into pieces and shove in clear cup or parfait dish. Two choices to make a quick and yummy dessert. Pour pudding over the cake in the dishes and chill.

A second choice would be to make gelatin and let it cool then pour over your cake in the dishes. Sometimes I use one cup juice and one cup water to make gelatin instead of the two cups of water on the directions. If using crushed pineapple then keep the juice to stir in. Spoon some whipped topping on the top before serving.

Snickers Cheesecake (Honey Lynch – Irish Assassin)

Like my job, this gives me pleasure. In my line of work you learn to follow steps in order to be successful. This recipe is no different. I just wanted you to know there really is a sweet side to me. Tierney James makes me out to be some kind of pyscho in *An Unlikely Hero* then again in *Knight Before Chaos*. I sort of redeemed myself in *Martyrs Never Die*.

Ingredients & Instructions

Crust:
3 T. butter, melted
1 ¼ c. graham cracker crumbs
1 T. sugar
Bake at 350 degrees for 10 minutes. Remove. Allow to cool.
3 pkgs. of 8oz. Cream cheese bars
3 eggs
¾ c. sugar
2 tsp. vanilla extract

2 Snickers, chopped

While it is cooling: Cream sugar and cream cheese until smooth. Add eggs, one at a time and vanilla. Next, stir in Snickers. Put into pan. Bake 45 minutes. Let cool then remove from pan.

Pumpkin Cheesecake (Honey Lynch – Irish Assassin)

Ingredients

1 ½ c. vanilla wafer crumbs
¾ c. sugar
¼ c. ground nuts (I use pecans)
¼ c. melted butter
2 (8 oz.) pkgs. cream cheese
1 c. pumpkin

¼ c. brown sugar
2 tsp. lemon juice
1 tsp. vanilla
1 carton frozen whipped topping thawed

Instructions

Preheat oven to 350 degrees.

Combine crumbs, ¼ c. granulated sugar, nuts and butter. Press into bottom of 9- or 10-inch pie plate. Bake in preheated oven for 5 minutes.

Beat cream cheese pumpkin, remaining ½ c. granulated sugar, brown sugar, lemon juice and vanilla until smooth. Fold in whipped topping.

Pour cheese mixture into crust. Chill at least 4 hours.

Apricot Velvet Cheese Cake (Honey Lynch – Irish Assassin)

Okay. So, I'm obsessed with cheesecake. My dear mum, gave me this recipe. I made it for some colorful folks I met in Belfast back in the day. They still remember me. I'm not sure it's for this cheesecake or maybe something else. You be the judge.

Ingredients

1 can 30-ounce apricots saving ½ c. of the syrup (Save 4-5 apricots for garnish at the end)
1 envelope unsweetened gelatin
2 pkgs. (8 oz.) cream cheese softened.
1 can (14 oz.) condensed milk
2 T. lemon juice
1 carton of (8 oz.) frozen whipped topping

Instructions

Combine ½ c. reserved syrup and gelatin. Stir over low heat until dissolved. Blend remaining apricot in blender on high. Combine apricot mixture to gelatin mixture. Fold in the whipped topping. Pour into no bake crust.
No Bake Crust
Combine the following and press into 9x13 pan.
1 Stick melted butter
1/3 c. sugar
1 ½ c. corn flake crumbs

Brownies To Die For – Sometimes it's worth it (Tessa)

Ingredients

¾ c. all-purpose flour
½ tsp. baking powder
¾ tsp. salt
2 eggs
1 c. sugar

1/3 c. oil
½ c. cocoa (Most of the time I use the instant chocolate you stir into milk for the kids.)
1 tsp. vanilla
¼ c. nuts (Use more if you like more pecans)

Instructions

Mix together and pour into a 9-inch square pan. Bake 350 degrees for 25-30 minutes. Cool. I add frosting on the top.

Fudge (Agent Willy Robbins of the Secret Service *Martyrs Never Die*)

Bring to a hard boil for 3 ½ minutes then turn off.
4 c sugar
1 large can of evaporated milk
1 stick butter
Add:
3 large Hershey bars
3 pkgs. of chocolate chips
3 c. pecans
1(8ounce jar) of marshmallow cream
Blend with other ingredients. When melted pour into buttered dish.
Makes 6 ½ pounds.

Irrational Dump Cake (Tessa)

Unfortunately, my reputation for sweets has gotten out of hand. At least once a week the Enigma team expects me to come waltzing in with something magical in the dessert department. My chocolate chip cookies used to be enough. Now they ask if I've heard of this recipe or how to make something called better than sex cake. (Guess who asked that? That's right. Samantha Cordova.)

The problem is I have a family to take care of. There's homework, laundry, mommy time, dance lessons, seasonal sports for the boys, church things—need I say more? The team saves the world then goes home to kick back and watch their favorite sporting event on TV or maybe go on a date for all I know. Yet they think I have time to satisfy their sweet tooth. Ugh! I tried quitting. But apparently making them fat and lazy is my super power. So, on those days I'm pressed for time and at my wit's end, I make something quick and easy with a hint of nutrition. Yeah, right.

Anyway, this is Irrational Dump Cake because it just shouldn't taste this good considering how easy it is. You'll find it in lots of places but they add crazy things that doesn't make it better. My recipe is simple and my momma taught me how to make it a long time ago.

Instructions

Spray a 9" x 13" dish with cooking spray. Preheat oven to 350 degrees.

Spread the following in the dish all the way to the edges.

1 (20 oz.) can cherry pie filling

1 (20 oz.) can crushed pineapple (leave a little juice at the bottom of the can)

1 box of white cake mix sprinkled on top of the fruit.

½ c. chopped pecans sprinkled on top of cake mix

Thinly slice two sticks of butter. (Don't you dare use margarine.) Place this on top of the pecans. Bake 45-50 minutes. Cool. Serve with butter pecan ice cream or your favorite whipped topping. It can sit on your kitchen counter if it isn't immediately consumed. On day two I usually place it in the refrigerator. Trust me. It doesn't last long. Even my kids love it. Pretty much explains why those grown kids with guns at Enigma like it too.

**My Guilty Pleasure Cake or Who Needs a Man Cake
(Agent Samantha Cordova)**

One bite and you'll know what I'm really talking about with this dessert. There's always a lot of moaning and eye rolling when guests eat this.

Ingredients

1 box Devil's food cake mix. Follow the directions to make it.
1 can (14 oz.) sweetened condensed milk
¾ c. caramel sauce (I buy the kind in a bottle for ice cream sundaes. Don't make this difficult.)
1 container of whipped topping
3 chocolate covered toffee candy bars chopped in small pieces

Instructions

Bake cake mix according to directions in a 13 x 9-inch pan. Then cool for 20 minutes until only warm to the touch. Using a fork, poke holes over entire cake, being careful not to push to bottom of cake. Next, you'll pour the condensed milk over the cake. To evenly coat the surface, I suggest you tilt the cake pan to be sure it fills the holes. Drizzle the caramel sauce over the top. After the cake cools to room temperature then refrigerate for at least two hours. If making ahead I'd refrigerate overnight. Just before serving spread a generous amount of whipped topping over the surface. Finish off with sprinkling the chopped toffee bars over the surface. Cut the cake into squares. Refrigeration is recommended for up to three days if all has not been consumed. Here is a little trick if you want to save some for later.

Give your guests small squares and stick the cake pan back in the refrigerator. Out of sight. Out of mind. Well, maybe not in this case, but they'll probably not ask for another piece if you don't have it on display for everyone to drool over.

Twinkie Cake (Agent Samantha Cordova)
Because I want to feed skinny girlfriends what they deserve.

12 Twinkie Cakes (any brand will do) and place in a 9 x 13 pan.

1 small box of Jell-O (I use strawberry). Make according to directions.

Pour the liquid over the cakes and let cool.

Prepare 1 box of vanilla pudding (any brand). I like the instant kind. Pour over your cakes and let set for about ten minutes or refrigerate if not using until later.

Finally baste the cakes with a large container of whipped topping. (Okay I'm really just smearing it on. It makes me feel empowered to pretend I'm basting a nutritious turkey. This is when it becomes a no guilt dessert.) Return to the refrigerator until ready to serve. To add a little humor, you can tell those skinny, yoga, members of a gym, always-on-a-diet, friends that if they eat this dessert standing up, there won't be any calories. They'll know you're kidding. (If they don't—oh well.) You'll be surprised how fast they gobble it down. While they're eating, dip some celery in a teaspoon of whipped topping and munch it where they can't see you.

Twinkie Cake 2.0 (Tessa)

I really like my version better than Sam's. This is a little more labor intensive but your guests will love it. Samantha thinks just walking into a room is enough for her guests.

Ingredients

1 box yellow cake mix
1 (3 oz.) box vanilla pudding
½ tsp. salt
1 c. water
1/3 c. vegetable oil
3 eggs

5 T. All-purpose flour
½ c. Crisco shortening
½ c. butter
1 c. sugar
2 tsp. vanilla
s

Instructions

Mix first six ingredients. Pour into a 9 x 13-inch pan lined with wax paper. Bake 35 minutes at 350 degrees. Cool cake completely and remove from pan. Slice the cake in half-length wise. Cook the flour and water in a saucepan until thick. Cool. Mix it with the rest of the ingredients. Beat with electric mixer for 8 minutes. Spread on top of the bottom half of the cake. Place top half on top of the filling. Adding a side of fresh strawberries makes it even better. Besides fresh fruit can make you feel better about eating something so decadent—or not. Maybe that's why you're eating it in the first place.

Apple or Peach Cobbler (Tessa)
When failure isn't an option.

Ingredients & Instructions

Preheat oven to 400 degrees. Cook 30-40 minutes.
Melt 1 stick butter in a 9 x 13 dish
Mix:
1 c. flour
1 c. sugar
Dash of salt
Heaping teaspoon baking powder
Pour 1 c. milk (not too full) to dry mix
Pour into butter
Add 4 c. fruit (pie filling will be easy to use) If you add unsweetened fruit, add an extra cup of sugar to the dry mix plus a dash of cinnamon.

Low Cal Chocolate Mousse (Honey Lynch)

Ingredients & Instructions

I box of Jell-O chocolate pudding mix, sugar free.
2 cups of 2% milk
1 container of frozen whipped cream, thawed
Mix Jell-O pudding and milk
Fold in one cup of whipped cream
Put in refrigerator for at least 30 minutes. Serve with dollops of remaining whipped cream.

Heather's Reindeer Food (Tessa's daughter)

She is convinced this is why Santa finds their house each year. According to her the reindeer appreciate they get the snack instead of Santa. Not sure if Captain Chase Hunter put that in her head when he was trying to explain the Virgin Mary at Christmas one year. The kids say to this day that was the best Christmas ever in spite of one blunder after another. You can find the whole story in *The Knight Before Chaos.* It's more like Home Alone meets Die Hard.

Ingredients

   1 pkg. vanilla almond bark
   1 box Golden Grahams cereal (any size)
   1-2 c. peanuts (We like the honey roasted)

Instructions

Melt almond bark according to package directions in large bowl. When almond bark is melted, dump in the cereal and nuts into bowl. Mix until coated completely. Pour out on foil and spread out evenly. Allow to cool and harden. When dry to the touch, break into chunks. Just remember to save some for the reindeer.

The Cracker Jack Boys (Daniel & Sean Patrick – Tessa's boys)

If you've read any of the Enigma Series you know these two are a hand full.

Ingredients

8 or 9 qt. popped corn
2 c. brown sugar
1 c. margarine or butter
1 tsp. salt

½ c. white syrup
1 tsp. vanilla
½ tsp. baking soda

Instructions

Boil all ingredients except the corn and baking soda for 5 minutes. Be sure to mix well and stir occasionally. Remove from heat and add the baking soda. Stir over corn. Place in oven at 250 degrees for on hour. Stir a couple of times. After the one hour, spread out flat surface covered with foil while still hot. This way you won't have a giant popcorn ball. I have added nuts to pretend there is a tiny bit of nutrition involved.

More Lies Tessa Tells Herself

When I decided to go to a geography conference in Washington DC I had no idea Enigma would be waiting for me. That scoundrel, Carter Johnson, flew the plane I took. Of course, I didn't know until I landed it was him. Needless to say, I freaked. I hadn't seen any of those sketchy agents for a year and when I saw two of them in the airport, I knew it was only a matter of time before my life would unravel. Between my uncle threatening the president and the Prime Minister of Israel, I didn't have a chance of a normal trip. Oh! And did I mention a hurricane barreled toward the Atlantic seaboard?

Layers of mayhem started to fall into place. I found myself at odds with Captain Hunter. Again.

One minute he was trying to find me before some Egyptian yahoos found me, the next he was pretending to undress me while luring them to come after us. Talk about an avalanche of emotions as to how I really felt about the captain, just managed to confuse me more.

It felt like we were growing closer. All those months apart weighed on me, wondering if he was safe, happy or even loved someone. I wanted him to believe in me, believe that I could stop the terrible thing my uncle planned to do to the president. But in the end I sided with Uncle Jake. It would be my undoing.

Being dragged into an alley by Captain Hunter to hide from Egyptian terrorists, cowering on a balcony from a possible bullet, with a former astronaut at my side, and Agent Samantha Cordova looking for an excuse to kill me, rounded out my trip to Washington DsC. All this because my uncle got it in his head, he needed to make a political statement about the attack on the USS Liberty by the Israelis in the mid-1960s.

The lies are stacking up and yet, my husband Robert remains clueless about this double life I've promised to keep secret. His big concern was being able to get his picture taken with the president. He has no idea *The Winds of Deception* was swritten by my friend Tierney James, was really about me. Maybe it's for the best.

ABOUT THE AUTHOR

Tierney James – Adventure, Thriller & Romantic Suspense Author

Tierney James decided to become a full-time writer after working in education for over thirty years. Besides serving as a Solar System Ambassador for NASA's Jet Propulsion Lab, and attending Space Camp for Educators, Tierney served as a Geo-teacher for National Geographic. Her love of travel and cultures took her on adventures throughout Africa, Asia and Europe. From the Great Wall of China to floating the Okavango Delta of Botswana, Tierney weaves her unique experiences into the adventures she loves to write. Living on a Native American reservation and in a mining town, fuels the characters in the Enigma and Wind Dancer series. Now with over twenty books under her belt, Tierney feels there is no stopping her now.

After moving to Oklahoma, the love of teaching continued in her marketing and writing workshops along with the creation of educational materials and children's books. She likes to tell people a little lipstick and danger makes the world go round. http://www.tierneyjames.com Speaking at conferences, book clubs, school functions, church and community groups are a few of the things Tierney enjoys doing when not writing her next adventure. She also helps beginning writers in their quest to become a published author through her workshops and classes. Family, an adopted dog and gardening fill her life with plenty of laughter to share with others.

Tierney has been an Amazon #1 Best Selling author and won numerous awards for her work.

OTHER PUBLICATIONS BY TIERNEY

Enigma Series
An Unlikely Hero
Winds of Deception
Rooftop Angels
Kifaru
Black Mamba
Knight Before Chaos
Invisible Goodbye
Martyrs Never Die

Novella
Secrets, Lies & Chocolate Chip Cookies

Education
How to Market a Book
African Safari – Thematic Lessons

Children's Books
There's a Superhero in the Library
Zombie Meatloaf
Mission K-9 Rescue

Dark Side Series
Dark Side of Morning
Dark Side of Noon

Lipstick & Danger Series
House of Miracles
The Rescued Heart

Stand Alone Books
Turnback Creek
Dance of the Devil's Trill
Lipstick and Danger -
Collection of Short Stories

FROM THE AUTHOR

Thanks for following along in each adventure I write. I'd love for you to follow me on social media as well.

Facebook: https://www.facebook.com/AuthorTierneyJames/

Facebook Reader Group:
https://www.facebook.com/groups/2430789897157949

Amazon:
https://www.amazon.com/Tierney-James/e/B00C1FB19Q

Twitter:
https://twitter.com/TierneyJames1

Website:
http://www.tierneyjames.com (Please sign up for my newsletter on the home page)

Pinterest:
https://www.pinterest.com/ptierneyjames/

Instagram:
www.tierneyjames7

NOTES

NOTES

NOTES

NOTES

NOTES

NOTES

* 9 7 8 1 9 6 5 4 6 0 3 5 1 *